‘Mind y
was a *pu*
respectable
opium-house,
and not one of
those stifling,
sweltering
chandoo-khanas
that you can find
all over the City.’

RUDYARD KIPLING

Born 1865, Bombay

Died 1936, London

All stories taken from *Plain Tales from the Hills*, first published in 1890

KIPLING IN PENGUIN CLASSICS

Captains Courageous

Just So Stories

Kim

Plain Tales from the Hills

Selected Poems

The Jungle Books

The Man Who Would Be King: Selected Stories

RUDYARD KIPLING

The Gate of the Hundred Sorrows

PENGUIN BOOKS

PENGUIN CLASSICS

Published by the Penguin Group
Penguin Books Ltd, 80 Strand, London WC2R 0RL, England
Penguin Group (USA) Inc., 375 Hudson Street, New York, New York 10014, USA
Penguin Group (Canada), 90 Eglinton Avenue East, Suite 700, Toronto, Ontario, Canada M4P 2Y3 (a division of Pearson Penguin Canada Inc.)
Penguin Ireland, 25 St Stephen's Green, Dublin 2, Ireland (a division of Penguin Books Ltd)
Penguin Group (Australia), 707 Collins Street, Melbourne, Victoria 3008, Australia (a division of Pearson Australia Group Pty Ltd)
Penguin Books India Pvt Ltd, 11 Community Centre, Panchsheel Park, New Delhi – 110 017, India
Penguin Group (NZ), 67 Apollo Drive, Rosedale, Auckland 0632, New Zealand (a division of Pearson New Zealand Ltd)
Penguin Books (South Africa) (Pty) Ltd, Block D, Rosebank Office Park, 181 Jan Smuts Avenue, Parktown North, Gauteng 2193, South Africa

Penguin Books Ltd, Registered Offices: 80 Strand, London WC2R 0RL, England

www.penguin.com

This selection published in Penguin Classics 2015
002

Set in 9/12.4 pt Baskerville 10 Pro
Typeset by Jouve (UK), Milton Keynes
Printed in Great Britain by Clays Ltd, St Ives plc

A CIP catalogue record for this book is available from the British Library

ISBN: 978-0-141-39806-8

www.greenpenguin.co.uk

Penguin Books is committed to a sustainable future for our business, our readers and our planet. This book is made from Forest Stewardship Council™ certified paper.

Contents

Thrown Away

And some are sulky, while some will plunge.
  (*So ho! Steady! Stand still, you!*)
Some you must gentle, and some you must lunge.
  (*There! There! Who wants to kill you?*)
Some – there are losses in every trade –
Will break their hearts ere bitted and made,
Will fight like fiends as the rope cuts hard,
And die dumb-mad in the breaking-yard.

Toolungala Stockyard Chorus

To rear a boy under what parents call the 'sheltered life' system is, if the boy must go into the world and fend for himself, not wise. Unless he be one in a thousand he has certainly to pass through many unnecessary troubles; and may, possibly, come to extreme grief simply from ignorance of the proper proportions of things.

Let a puppy eat the soap in the bath-room or chew a newly-blacked boot. He chews and chuckles until, by and by, he finds out that blacking and Old Brown Windsor make him very sick. So he argues that soap and boots are not wholesome. Any old dog about the house will soon show him the unwisdom of biting big dogs' ears. Being young, he remembers, and goes abroad, at six months, a well-mannered little beast with a chastened appetite. If he had been kept away from boots, and soap, and big dogs till he came to the trinity full-grown and with developed teeth, consider how fearfully sick and thrashed he would be! Apply that notion to the 'sheltered life', and see how it works. It does not sound pretty, but it is the better of two evils.

There was a Boy once who had been brought up under the 'sheltered life' theory; and the theory killed him dead. He stayed with his people all his days, from the hour he was born till the hour he went into Sandhurst nearly at the top of the list. He was beautifully taught in all that wins marks by a private tutor, and carried the extra weight of 'never having given his parents an hour's anxiety in his life'. What he learnt at Sandhurst beyond the regular routine is of no great consequence. He looked about him, and he found soap and blacking, so to speak, very good. He ate a little, and came out of Sandhurst not so high as he went in. Then there was an interval and a scene with his people, who expected much from him. Next a year of living unspotted from the world in a third-rate depôt battalion where all the juniors were children and all the seniors old women; and lastly, he came out to India, where he was cut off from the support of his parents, and had no one to fall back on in time of trouble except himself.

Now India is a place beyond all others where one must not take things too seriously – the mid-day sun always excepted. Too much work and too much energy kill a man just as effectively as too much assorted vice or too much drink. Flirtation does not matter, because every one is being transferred, and either you or she leave the station and never return. Good work does not matter, because a man is judged by his worst output, and another man takes all the credit of his best as a rule. Bad work does not matter, because other men do worse, and incompetents hang on longer in India than anywhere else. Amusements do not matter, because you must repeat them as soon as you have accomplished them once, and most amusements only mean trying to win another person's money. Sickness does not matter, because it's all in the day's work, and if you die, another man takes over your place and your office in the eight hours between your death and burial. Nothing matters except Home-furlough and acting allowances, and these only because they are scarce. It is a slack country, where all men work with imperfect instruments, and the wisest thing is to escape as soon as ever you can to some place where amusement is amusement and a reputation worth the having.

But this Boy – the tale is as old as the Hills – came out, and took all things seriously. He was pretty and was petted. He took the pettings seriously, and fretted over women not worth saddling a pony to call upon. He found his new free life in India very good. It *does* look attractive in the beginning, from a subaltern's point of view – all ponies, partners, dancing, and so on. He tasted it as the puppy tastes the soap. Only he came late to the eating, with a grown set of teeth. He had no sense of balance – just like the puppy – and could not understand why he was not treated with the consideration he received under his father's roof. That hurt his feelings.

He quarrelled with other boys and, being sensitive to the marrow, remembered these quarrels, and they excited him.

He found whist, and gymkhanas, and things of that kind (meant to amuse one after office) good; but he took them seriously too, just as seriously as he took the 'head' that followed after drink. He lost his money over whist and gymkhanas because they were new to him.

He took his losses seriously, and wasted as much energy and interest over a two-goldmohur race for maiden *ekka*-ponies with their manes hogged, as if it had been the Derby. One-half of this came from inexperience – much as the puppy squabbles with the corner of the hearthrug – and the other half from the dizziness bred by stumbling out of his quiet life into the glare and excitement of a livelier one. No one told him about the soap and the blacking, because an average man takes it for granted that an average man is ordinarily careful in regard to them. It was pitiful to watch The Boy knocking himself to pieces, as an over-handled colt falls down and cuts himself when he gets away from his groom.

This unbridled licence in amusements not worth the trouble of breaking line for, much less rioting over, endured for six months – all through one cold weather – and then we thought that the heat and the knowledge of having lost his money and health and lamed his horses would sober The Boy down, and he would stand steady. In ninety-nine cases out of a hundred this would have happened. You can see the principle working in any Indian station. But this particular case fell through because The Boy was sensitive and took things seriously – as I may have said some seven times before. Of course, we could not tell how his excesses struck him personally. They were nothing very heartbreaking or above the average. He might be crippled for life financially, and want a little nursing. Still, the memory of his performances would wither away in one hot weather, and the bankers would help him to tide over the money-troubles. But he must have taken another view altogether, and have believed himself ruined beyond redemption. His Colonel talked to him severely when the cold weather ended. That made him more wretched than ever; and it was only an ordinary 'Colonel's wigging'!

What follows is a curious instance of the fashion in which we are all linked together and made responsible for one another. *The* thing that kicked the beam in The Boy's mind was a remark that a woman made when he was talking to her. There is no use in repeating it, for it was only a cruel little sentence, rapped out before thinking, that made him flush to the roots of his hair. He kept himself to himself for three days, and then put in for two days' leave to go shooting near a Canal Engineer's Rest House about thirty miles out. He got his leave, and that night at Mess was noisier and more offensive than ever. He said that he was 'going to shoot big game', and left at half-past ten o'clock in an *ekka*. Partridge – which was the only thing a man could get near the Rest House – is not big game; so every one laughed.

Next morning one of the Majors came in from short leave, and heard that The Boy had gone out to shoot 'big game'. The Major had taken an interest in The Boy, and had, more than once, tried to check him. The Major put up his eyebrows when he heard of the expedition, and went to The Boy's rooms, where he rummaged.

Presently he came out and found me leaving cards on the Mess. There was no one else in the ante-room.

He said, 'The Boy has gone out shooting. *Does* a man shoot partridge with a revolver and writing-case?'

I said, 'Nonsense, Major!' for I saw what was in his mind.

He said, 'Nonsense or no nonsense, I'm going to the Canal now – at once. I don't feel easy.'

Then he thought for a minute, and said, 'Can you lie?'

'You know best,' I answered. 'It's my profession.'

'Very well,' said the Major, 'you come out with me now – at once – in an *ekka* to the Canal to shoot black-buck. Go and put on *shikar*-kit – *quick* – and drive here with a gun.'

The Major was a masterful man, and I knew that he would not give orders for nothing. So I obeyed, and on return found the Major packed up in an *ekka* – gun-cases and food slung below – all ready for a shooting-trip.

He dismissed the driver and drove himself. We jogged along quietly while in the station; but, as soon as we got to the dusty road across the plains, he made that pony fly. A country-bred can do nearly anything at a pinch. We covered the thirty miles in under three hours, but the poor brute was nearly dead.

Once I said, 'What's the blazing hurry, Major?'

He said quietly, 'The Boy has been alone, by himself for – one, two, five, – fourteen hours now! I tell you, I don't feel easy.'

This uneasiness spread itself to me, and I helped to beat the pony.

When we came to the Canal Engineer's Rest House the Major called for The Boy's servant; but there was no answer. Then we went up to the house, calling for The Boy by name; but there was no answer.

'Oh, he's out shooting,' said I.

Just then I saw through one of the windows a little hurricane-lamp burning. This was at four in the afternoon. We both stopped dead in the veranda, holding our breath to catch every sound; and we heard, inside the room, the '*brr – brr – brr*' of a multitude of flies. The Major said nothing, but he took off his helmet and we entered very softly.

The Boy was dead on the bed in the centre of the bare, lime-washed room. He had shot his head nearly to pieces with his revolver. The gun-cases were still strapped, so was the bedding, and on the table lay The Boy's writing-case with photographs. He had gone away to die like a poisoned rat!

The Major said to himself softly, 'Poor Boy! Poor, *poor* devil!' Then he turned away from the bed and said, 'I want your help in this business.'

Knowing The Boy was dead by his own hand, I saw exactly what that help would be, so I passed over to the table, took a chair, lit a cheroot, and began to go through the writing-case; the Major looking over my shoulder and repeating to himself, 'We came too late! – Like a rat in a hole! – Poor, *poor* devil!'

The Boy must have spent half the night in writing to his people, to his Colonel, and to a girl at Home; and as soon as he had finished, must have shot himself, for he had been dead a long time when we came in.

I read all that he had written, and passed over each sheet to the Major as I finished it.

We saw from his accounts how very seriously he had taken everything. He wrote about 'disgrace which he was unable to bear' – 'indelible shame' – 'criminal folly' – 'wasted life', and so on; besides a lot of private things to his father and mother much too sacred to put into print. The letter to the girl at Home was the most pitiful of all, and I choked as I read it. The Major made no attempt to keep dry-eyed. I respected him for that. He read and rocked himself to and fro, and simply cried like a woman without caring to hide it. The letters were so dreary and hopeless and touching. We forgot all about The Boy's follies, and only thought of the poor Thing on the bed and the scrawled sheets in our hands. It was utterly impossible to let the letters go Home. They would have broken his father's heart and killed his mother after killing her belief in her son.

At last the Major dried his eyes openly, and said, 'Nice sort of thing to spring on an English family! What shall we do?'

I said, knowing what the Major had brought me out for, 'The Boy died of cholera. We were with him at the time. We can't commit ourselves to half-measures. Come along.'

Then began one of the most grimly comic scenes I have ever taken part in – the concoction of a big, written lie, bolstered with evidence to soothe The Boy's people at Home. I began the rough draft of the letter, the Major throwing in hints here and there while he gathered up all the stuff that The Boy had written and burnt it in the fireplace. It was a hot, still evening when we began, and the lamp burned very badly. In due course I made the draft to my satisfaction, setting forth how The Boy was the pattern of all virtues, beloved by his Regiment, with every promise of a great career before him, and so on; how we had helped him through the sickness – it was no time for little lies, you will understand – and how he had died without pain. I choked while I was putting down these things and thinking of the poor people who would read them. Then I laughed at the grotesqueness of the affair, and the laughter mixed itself up with the choke – and the Major said that we both wanted drinks.

I am afraid to say how much whisky we drank before the letter was finished. It had not the least effect on us. Then we took off The Boy's watch, locket, and ring.

Lastly, the Major said, 'We must send a lock of hair too. A woman values that.'

But there were reasons why we could not find a lock fit to send. The Boy was black-haired, and so was the Major, luckily. I cut off a piece of the Major's hair above the temple with a knife, and put it into the packet we were making. The laughing-fit and the chokes got hold of me again, and I had to stop. The Major was nearly as bad; and we both knew that the worst part of the work was to come.

We sealed up the packet, photographs, locket, seals, ring, letter, and lock of hair with The Boy's sealing-wax and The Boy's seal.

Then the Major said, 'For God's sake, let's get outside – away from the room – and think!'

We went outside, and walked on the banks of the Canal for an hour, eating and drinking what we had with us, until the moon rose. I know now exactly how a murderer feels. Finally, we forced ourselves back to the room with the lamp and the Other Thing in it, and began to take up the next piece of work. I am not going to write about this. It was too horrible. We burned the bedstead and dropped the ashes into the Canal; we took up the matting of the room and treated that in the same way. I went off to a village and borrowed two big hoes, – I did not want the villagers to help, – while the Major arranged – the other matters. It took us four hours' hard work to make the grave. As we worked, we argued out whether it was right to say as much as we remembered of the Burial of the Dead. We compromised things by saying the Lord's Prayer with a private unofficial prayer for the peace of the soul of The Boy. Then we filled in the grave and went into the veranda – not the house – to lie down to sleep. We were dead tired.

When we woke the Major said wearily, 'We can't go back till to-morrow. We must give him a decent time to die in. He died early *this* morning, remember. That seems more natural.' So the Major must have been lying awake all the time, thinking.

I said, 'Then why didn't we bring the body back to cantonments?'

The Major thought for a minute. 'Because the people bolted when they heard of the cholera. And the *ekka* has gone!'

That was strictly true. We had forgotten all about the *ekka*-pony, and he had gone home.

So we were left there alone, all that stifling day, in the Canal Rest House, testing and re-testing our story of The Boy's death to see if it was weak in any point. A native appeared in the afternoon, but we said that a Sahib was dead of cholera, and he ran away. As the dusk gathered, the Major told me all his fears about The Boy, and awful stories of suicide or nearly-carried-out suicide – tales that made one's hair crisp. He said that he himself had once gone into the same Valley of the Shadow as The Boy, when he was young and new to the country; so he understood how things fought together in The Boy's poor jumbled head. He also said that youngsters, in their repentant moments, consider their sins much more serious and ineffaceable than they really are. We talked together all through the evening and rehearsed the story of the death of The Boy. As soon as the moon was up, and The Boy, theoretically, just buried, we struck across country for the station. We walked from eight till six o'clock in the morning; but though we were dead tired, we did not forget to go to The Boy's rooms and put away his revolver with the proper amount of cartridges in the pouch. Also to set his writing-case on the table. We found the Colonel and reported the death, feeling more like murderers than ever. Then we went to bed and slept the clock round, for there was no more in us.

The tale had credence as long as was necessary; for every one forgot about The Boy before a fortnight was over. Many people, however, found time to say that the Major had behaved scandalously in not bringing in the body for a Regimental funeral. The saddest thing of all was the letter from The Boy's mother to the Major and me – with big inky blisters all over the sheet. She wrote the sweetest possible things about our great kindness, and the obligation she would be under to us as long as she lived.

All things considered, she was under an obligation, but not exactly as she meant.

False Dawn

To-night, God knows what thing shall tide,
  The Earth is racked and fain –
Expectant, sleepless, open-eyed;
And we, who from the Earth were made,
  Thrill with our Mother's pain.

In Durance

No man will ever know the exact truth of this story; though women may sometimes whisper it to one another after a dance, when they are putting up their hair for the night and comparing lists of victims. A man, of course, cannot assist at these functions. So the tale must be told from the outside – in the dark – all wrong.

Never praise a sister to a sister, in the hope of your compliments reaching the proper ears, and so preparing the way for you later on. Sisters are women first, and sisters afterwards; and you will find that you do yourself harm.

Saumarez knew this when he made up his mind to propose to the elder Miss Copleigh. Saumarez was a strange man, with few merits so far as men could see, though he was popular with women, and carried enough conceit to stock a Viceroy's Council and leave a little over for the Commander-in-Chief's Staff. He was a Civilian. Very many women took an interest in Saumarez, perhaps because his manner to them was offensive. If you hit a pony over the nose at the outset of your acquaintance, he may not love you, but he will take a deep interest in your movements ever afterwards. The elder Miss Copleigh was nice, plump, winning, and pretty. The younger was not so pretty, and, from men disregarding the hint set forth above, her style was repellent and unattractive. Both girls had, practically, the same figure, and there was a strong likeness between them in look and voice; though no one could doubt for an instant which was the nicer of the two.

Saumarez made up his mind, as soon as they came into the station from Behar, to marry the elder one. At least, we all made sure that he would, which comes to the same thing. She was two-and-twenty, and he was thirty-three, with pay and allowances of nearly fourteen hundred rupees a month. So the match, as we arranged it, was in every way a good one. Saumarez was his name, and summary was his nature, as a man once said. Having drafted his Resolution, he formed a Select Committee of One to sit upon it, and resolved to take his time. In our unpleasant slang, the Copleigh girls 'hunted in couples'. That is to say, you could do nothing with one without the other. They were very loving sisters; but their mutual affection was sometimes inconvenient. Saumarez held the balance hair-true between them, and none but himself could have said to which side his heart inclined, though every one guessed. He rode with them a good deal and danced with them, but he never succeeded in detaching them from each other for any length of time.

Women said that the two girls kept together through deep

mistrust, each fearing that the other would steal a march on her. But that has nothing to do with a man. Saumarez was silent for good or bad, and as business-likely attentive as he could be, having due regard to his work and his polo. Beyond doubt both girls were fond of him.

As the hot weather drew nearer and Saumarez made no sign, women said that you could see their trouble in the eyes of the girls – that they were looking strained, anxious, and irritable. Men are quite blind in these matters unless they have more of the woman than the man in their composition; in which case it does not matter what they say or think. I maintain it was the hot April days that took the colour out of the Copleigh girls' cheeks. They should have been sent to the Hills early. No one – man or woman – feels an angel when the hot weather is approaching. The younger sister grew more cynical, not to say acid, in her ways; and the winningness of the elder wore thin. There was effort in it.

The station wherein all these things happened was, though not a little one, off the line of rail, and suffered through want of attention. There were no Gardens or bands or amusements worth speaking of, and it was nearly a day's journey to come into Lahore for a dance. People were grateful for small things to interest them.

About the beginning of May, and just before the final exodus of Hill-goers, when the weather was very hot and there were not more than twenty people in the station, Saumarez gave a moonlight riding-picnic at an old tomb, six miles away, near the bed of the river. It was a 'Noah's Ark' picnic; and there was to be the usual arrangement of quarter-mile intervals between each couple on account of the dust. Six couples came altogether, including chaperons. Moonlight picnics are useful just at the very end of the season, before all the girls go away to the Hills. They lead to understandings, and should be encouraged by chaperons, especially those whose girls look sweetest in riding-habits. I knew a case once . . . But that is another story. That picnic was called the 'Great Pop Picnic', because every one knew Saumarez would propose then to the elder Miss Copleigh; and, besides his affair, there was another which might possibly come to happiness. The social atmosphere was heavily charged and wanted clearing.

We met at the parade-ground at ten. The night was fearfully hot. The horses sweated even at walking-pace, but anything was better than sitting still in our own dark houses. When we moved off under the full moon we were four couples, one triplet, and Me. Saumarez rode with the Copleigh girls, and I loitered at the tail of the procession wondering with whom Saumarez would ride home. Every one was happy and contented; but we all felt that things were going to happen. We rode slowly; and it was nearly midnight before we reached the old tomb, facing the ruined tank, in the decayed gardens where we were going to eat and drink. I was late in coming up; and, before I went into the garden, I saw that the horizon to the north carried a faint, dun-coloured feather. But no one would have thanked me for spoiling so well-managed an entertainment as this picnic – and a dust-storm, more or less, does no great harm.

We gathered by the tank. Some one had brought out a banjo – which is a most sentimental instrument – and three or four of us sang. You must not laugh at this. Our amusements in out-of-the-way stations are very few indeed. Then we talked in groups or together, lying under the trees, with the sun-baked roses dropping their petals on our feet, until supper was ready. It was a beautiful supper, as cold and as iced as you could wish; and we stayed long over it.

I had felt that the air was growing hotter and hotter; but nobody seemed to notice it until the moon went out and a burning hot wind began lashing the orange-trees with a sound like the noise of the sea. Before we knew where we were the dust-storm was on us, and everything was roaring, whirling darkness. The supper-table was blown bodily into the tank. We were afraid of staying anywhere near the old tomb for fear it might be blown down. So we felt our way to the orange-trees where the horses were picketed and waited for the storm to blow over. Then the little light that was left vanished, and you could not see your hand before your face. The air was heavy with dust and sand from the bed of the river, that filled boots and pockets, and drifted down necks, and coated eyebrows and moustaches. It was one of the worst dust-storms of the year. We were all huddled together close to the trembling horses, with the thunder chattering overhead, and the lightning spurting like water from a sluice, all ways at once. There was no danger, of course, unless the horses broke loose. I was standing with my head down wind and my hands over my mouth, hearing the trees thrashing each other. I could not see who was next me till the flashes came. Then I found that I was packed near Saumarez and the elder Miss Copleigh, with my own horse just in front of me. I recognized the elder Miss Copleigh, because she had a *pagri* round her helmet, and the younger had not. All the electricity in the air had gone into my body, and I was quivering and tingling from head to foot – exactly as a corn shoots and tingles before rain. It was a grand storm. The wind seemed to be picking up the earth and pitching it to leeward in great heaps, and the heat beat up from the ground like the heat of the Day of Judgment.

The storm lulled slightly after the first half-hour, and I heard a despairing little voice close to my ear, saying to itself, quietly and softly, as if some lost soul were flying about with the wind, 'Oh, my God!' Then the younger Miss Copleigh stumbled into my arms, saying, 'Where is my horse? Get my horse. I want to go home. I want to go home. Take me home.'

I thought that the lightning and the black darkness had frightened her. So I said there was no danger, but she must wait till the storm blew over. She answered, 'It is not that! I want to go home! Oh, take me away from here!'

I said that she could not go till the light came; but I felt her brush past me and go away. It was too dark to see where. Then the whole sky was split open with one tremendous flash, as if the end of the world were coming, and all the women shrieked.

Almost directly after this I felt a man's hand on my shoulder, and heard Saumarez bellowing in my ear. Through the rattling of the trees and howling of the wind I did not catch his words at once, but at last I heard him say, 'I've proposed to the wrong one! What shall I do?' Saumarez had no occasion to make this confidence to me. I was never a friend of his, nor am I now; but I fancy neither of us were ourselves just then. He was shaking as he stood with excitement, and

I was feeling queer all over with the electricity. I could not think of anything to say except, 'More fool you for proposing in a dust-storm.' But I did not see how that would improve the mistake.

Then he shouted, 'Where's Edith – Edith Copleigh?' Edith was the younger sister. I answered out of my astonishment, 'What do you want with *her*?' For the next two minutes he and I were shouting at each other like maniacs, – he vowing that it was the younger sister he had meant to propose to all along, and I telling him, till my throat was hoarse, that he must have made a mistake! I cannot account for this except, again, by the fact that we were neither of us ourselves. Everything seemed to me like a bad dream – from the stamping of the horses in the darkness to Saumarez telling me the story of his loving Edith Copleigh from the first. He was still clawing my shoulder and begging me to tell him where Edith Copleigh was, when another lull came and brought light with it, and we saw the dust-cloud forming on the plain in front of us. So we knew the worst was over. The moon was low down, and there was just the glimmer of the false dawn that comes about an hour before the real one. But the light was very faint, and the dun cloud roared like a bull. I wondered where Edith Copleigh had gone; and as I was wondering I saw three things together: First, Maud Copleigh's face come smiling out of the darkness and move towards Saumarez who was standing by me. I heard the girl whisper, 'George,' and slide her arm through the arm that was not clawing my shoulder, and I saw that look on her face which only comes once or twice in a lifetime – when a woman is perfectly happy and the air is full of trumpets and gorgeously-coloured fire, and the Earth turns into cloud because she loves and is loved. At the same time, I saw Saumarez's face as he heard Maud Copleigh's voice, and, fifty yards away from the clump of orange-trees, I saw a brown holland habit getting upon a horse.

It must have been my state of over-excitement that made me so ready to meddle with what did not concern me. Saumarez was moving off to the habit; but I pushed him back and said, 'Stop here and explain. I'll fetch her back!' And I ran out to get at my own horse. I had a perfectly unnecessary notion that everything must be done decently and in order, and that Saumarez's first care was to wipe the happy look out of Maud Copleigh's face. All the time I was linking up the curb-chain I wondered how he would do it.

I cantered after Edith Copleigh, thinking to bring her back slowly on some pretence or another. But she galloped away as soon as she saw me, and I was forced to ride after her in earnest. She called back over her shoulder, 'Go away! I'm going home. Oh, go away!' two or three times; but my business was to catch her first, and argue later. The ride fitted in with the rest of the evil dream. The ground was very rough, and now and again we rushed through the whirling, choking 'dust-devils' in the skirts of the flying storm. There was a burning hot wind blowing that brought up a stench of stale brick-kilns with it; and through the half-light and through the dust-devils, across that desolate plain, flickered the brown holland habit on the grey horse. She headed for the station at first. Then she wheeled round and set off for the river through beds of burnt-down jungle-grass, bad even to ride pig over. In cold blood I should never have dreamed of going over such a country at night, but it seemed quite right and natural with the lightning crackling overhead, and a reek like the smell of the Pit in my nostrils. I rode and shouted, and she bent forward and lashed her horse, and the aftermath of the dust-storm came up, and caught us both, and drove us down wind like pieces of paper.

I don't know how far we rode; but the drumming of the horse-hoofs and the roar of the wind and the race of the faint blood-red moon through the yellow mist seemed to have gone on for years and years, and I was literally drenched with sweat from my helmet to my gaiter when the grey stumbled, recovered himself, and pulled up dead lame. My brute was used up altogether. Edith Copleigh was bareheaded, plastered with dust, and crying bitterly. 'Why can't you let me alone?' she said. 'I only wanted to get away and go home. Oh, *please* let me go!'

'You have got to come back with me, Miss Copleigh. Saumarez has something to say to you.'

It was a foolish way of putting it; but I hardly knew Miss Copleigh, and, though I was playing Providence at the cost of my horse, I could not tell her in as many words what Saumarez had told me. I thought he could do that better himself. All her pretence about being tired and wanting to go home broke down, and she rocked herself to and fro in the saddle as she sobbed, and the hot wind blew her black hair to leeward. I am not going to repeat what she said, because she was utterly unstrung.

This was the cynical Miss Copleigh, and I, almost an utter stranger to her, was trying to tell her that Saumarez loved her, and she was to come back to hear him say so. I believe

I made myself understood, for she gathered the grey together and made him hobble somehow, and we set off for the tomb, while the storm went thundering down to Umballa and a few big drops of warm rain fell. I found out that she had been standing close to Saumarez when he proposed to her sister, and had wanted to go home to cry in peace, as an English girl should. She dabbed her eyes with her pocket-handkerchief as we went along, and babbled to me out of sheer lightness of heart and hysteria. That was perfectly unnatural; and yet it seemed all right at the time and in the place. All the world was only the two Copleigh girls, Saumarez, and I, ringed in with the lightning and the dark; and the guidance of this misguided world seemed to lie in my hands.

When we returned to the tomb in the deep, dead stillness that followed the storm, the dawn was just breaking and nobody had gone away. They were waiting for our return. Saumarez most of all. His face was white and drawn. As Miss Copleigh and I limped up, he came forward to meet us, and, when he helped her down from her saddle, he kissed her before all the picnic. It was like a scene in a theatre, and the likeness was heightened by all the dust-white, ghostly-looking men and women under the orange-trees clapping their hands – as if they were watching a play – at Saumarez's choice. I never knew anything so un-English in my life.

Lastly, Saumarez said we must all go home or the station would come out to look for us, and would I be good enough to ride home with Maud Copleigh? Nothing would give me greater pleasure, I said.

So we formed up, six couples in all, and went back two

by two; Saumarez walking at the side of Edith Copleigh, who was riding his horse. Maud Copleigh did not talk to me at any length.

The air was cleared; and, little by little, as the sun rose, I felt we were all dropping back again into ordinary men and women, and that the 'Great Pop Picnic' was a thing altogether a part and out of the world – never to happen again. It had gone with the dust-storm and the tingle in the hot air.

I felt tired and limp, and a good deal ashamed of myself, as I went in for a bath and some sleep.

There is a woman's version of this story, but it will never be written . . . unless Maud Copleigh cares to try.

In the House of Suddhoo

A stone's throw out on either hand
From that well-ordered road we tread,
  And all the world is wild and strange:
Churel and ghoul and *Djinn* and sprite
Shall bear us company to-night,
For we have reached the Oldest Land
  Wherein the Powers of Darkness range.

From the Dusk to the Dawn

The house of Suddhoo, near the Taksali Gate, is two-storeyed, with four carved windows of old brown wood, and a flat roof. You may recognize it by five red hand-prints arranged like the Five of Diamonds on the whitewash between the upper windows. Bhagwan Dass the grocer and a man who says he gets his living by seal-cutting live in the lower storey with a troop of wives, servants, friends, and retainers. The two upper rooms used to be occupied by Janoo and Azizun, and a little black-and-tan terrier that was stolen from an Englishman's house and given to Janoo by a soldier. To-day, only Janoo lives in the upper rooms. Suddhoo sleeps on the roof generally, except when he sleeps in the street. He used to go to Peshawur in the cold weather to visit his son who sells curiosities near the Edwardes' Gate, and then he slept under a real mud roof. Suddhoo is a great friend of mine, because his cousin had a son who secured, thanks to my recommendation, the post of head-messenger to a big firm in the station. Suddhoo says that God will make me a Lieutenant-Governor one of these days. I daresay his prophecy will come true. He is very, very old, with white hair and no teeth worth showing, and he has outlived his wits – outlived nearly everything except his fondness for his son at Peshawur. Janoo and Azizun are Kashmiris, Ladies of the City, and theirs was an ancient and more or less honourable profession; but Azizun has since married a medical student from the North-West and has settled down to a most respectable life somewhere near Bareilly. Bhagwan Dass is an extortioner and an adulterator. He is very rich. The man who is supposed to get his living by seal-cutting pretends to be poor. This lets you know as much as is necessary of the four principal tenants in the house of Suddhoo. Then there is Me, of course; but I am only the chorus that comes in at the end to explain things. So I do not count.

Suddhoo was not clever. The man who pretended to cut seals was the cleverest of them all – Bhagwan Dass only knew how to lie – except Janoo. She was also beautiful, but that was her own affair.

Suddhoo's son at Peshawur was attacked by pleurisy, and old Suddhoo was troubled. The seal-cutter man heard of Suddhoo's anxiety and made capital out of it. He was abreast of the times. He got a friend in Peshawur to telegraph daily accounts of the son's health. And here the story begins.

Suddhoo's cousin's son told me, one evening, that Suddhoo wanted to see me; that he was too old and feeble to come personally, and that I should be conferring an everlasting honour on the House of Suddhoo if I went to him. I went; but I think, seeing how well off Suddhoo was then, that he might have sent something better than an *ekka*, which jolted fearfully, to haul out a future Lieutenant-Governor to the City on a muggy April evening. The *ekka* did not run quickly. It was full dark when we pulled up opposite the door of Ranjit Singh's Tomb near the main gate of the Fort. Here was Suddhoo, and he said that by reason of my condescension, it was absolutely certain that I should become a Lieutenant-Governor while my hair was yet black. Then we talked about the weather and the state of my health, and the wheat crops, for fifteen minutes, in the Huzuri Bagh, under the stars.

Suddhoo came to the point at last. He said that Janoo had told him that there was an order of the Sirkar against magic, because it was feared that magic might one day kill the Empress of India. I didn't know anything about the state of the law; but I fancied that something interesting was going to happen. I said that so far from magic being discouraged by the Government, it was highly commended. The greatest officials of the State practised it themselves. (If the Financial Statement isn't magic, I don't know what is.) Then, to encourage him further, I said that, if there was any *jadoo* afoot, I had not the least objection to giving it my countenance and sanction, and to seeing that it was clean *jadoo* – white magic, as distinguished from the unclean *jadoo* which kills folk. It took a long time before Suddhoo admitted that this was just what he had asked me to come for. Then he told me, in jerks and quavers, that the man who said he cut seals was a sorcerer of the cleanest kind; that every day he gave Suddhoo news of the sick son in Peshawur more quickly than the lightning could fly, and that this news was always corroborated by the letters. Further, that he had told Suddhoo how a great danger was threatening his son, which could be removed by clean *jadoo*; and, of course, heavy payment. I began to see exactly how the land lay, and told Suddhoo that I also understood a little *jadoo* in the Western line, and would go to his house to see that everything was done decently and in order. We set off together; and on the way Suddhoo told me that he had paid the seal-cutter between one hundred and two hundred rupees already; and the *jadoo* of that night would cost two hundred more. Which was cheap, he said, considering the greatness of his son's danger; but I do not think he meant it.

The lights were all cloaked in the front of the house when we arrived. I could hear awful noises from behind the seal-cutter's shop-front, as if some one were groaning his soul out. Suddhoo shook all over, and while we groped our way upstairs told me that the *jadoo* had begun. Janoo and Azizun met us at the stair-head, and told us that the *jadoo*-work was coming off in their rooms, because there was more space there. Janoo is a lady of a free-thinking turn of mind. She whispered that the *jadoo* was an invention to get money out of Suddhoo, and that the seal-cutter would go to a hot place when he died. Suddhoo was nearly crying with fear and old age. He kept walking up and down the room in the half-light, repeating his son's name over and over again, and asking Azizun if the seal-cutter ought not to make a reduction in the case of his own landlord. Janoo pulled me over to the shadow in the recess of the carved bow-windows. The boards were up, and the rooms were only lit by one tiny oil-lamp. There was no chance of my being seen if I stayed still.

Presently, the groans below ceased, and we heard steps on the staircase. That was the seal-cutter. He stopped outside the door as the terrier barked and Azizun fumbled at the chain, and he told Suddhoo to blow out the lamp. This left the place in jet darkness, except for the red glow from the two hookahs that belonged to Janoo and Azizun. The seal-cutter came in, and I heard Suddhoo throw himself down on the floor and groan. Azizun caught her breath, and Janoo backed on to one of the beds with a shudder. There was a clink of something metallic, and then shot up a pale blue-green flame near the ground. The light was just enough to show Azizun, pressed against one corner of the room with the terrier between her knees; Janoo, with her hands clasped, leaning forward as she sat on the bed; Suddhoo, face-down, quivering, and the seal-cutter.

I hope I may never see another man like that seal-cutter. He was stripped to the waist, with a wreath of white jasmine as thick as my wrist round his forehead, a salmon-coloured loin-cloth round his middle, and a steel bangle on each ankle. This was not awe-inspiring. It was the face of the man that turned me cold. It was blue-grey in the first place. In the second, the eyes were rolled back till you could see the whites of them; and, in the third, the face was the face of a demon – a ghoul – anything you please except of the sleek, oily old ruffian who sat in the daytime over his turning-lathe downstairs. He was lying on his stomach with his arms turned and crossed behind him, as if he had been thrown down pinioned. His head and neck were the only parts of him off the floor. They were nearly at right angles to the body, like the head of a cobra at spring. It was ghastly. In the centre of the room, on the bare earth floor, stood a big, deep, brass basin, with a pale blue-green light floating in the centre like a night-light. Round that basin the man on the floor wriggled himself three times. How he did it I do not know. I could see the muscles ripple along his spine and fall smooth again; but I could not see any other motion. The head seemed the only thing alive about him, except that slow curl and uncurl of the labouring back-muscles. Janoo from the bed was breathing seventy to the minute; Azizun held her hands before her eyes; and old Suddhoo, fingering at the dirt that had got into his white beard, was crying to himself. The horror of it was that the creeping, crawly thing made no sound – only crawled! And, remember, this lasted for ten minutes, while the terrier whined, and Azizun shuddered, and Janoo gasped, and Suddhoo cried!

I felt the hair lift at the back of my head, and my heart thump like a thermantidote-paddle. Luckily, the seal-cutter betrayed himself by his most impressive trick and made me calm again. After he had finished that unspeakable triple crawl, he stretched his head away from the floor as high as he could, and sent out a jet of fire from his nostrils. Now, I knew how fire-spouting is done – I can do it myself – so I felt at ease. The business was a fraud. If he had only kept to that crawl without trying to raise the effect, goodness knows what I might not have thought. Both the girls shrieked at the jet of fire, and the head dropped, chin down on the floor, with a thud; the whole body lying there like a corpse with its arms trussed. There was a pause of five full minutes after this, and the blue-green flame died down. Janoo stooped to settle one of her anklets, while Azizun turned her face to the wall and took the terrier in her arms. Suddhoo put out an arm mechanically to Janoo's hookah, and she slid it across the floor with her foot. Directly above the body and on the wall were a couple of flaming portraits, in stamped-paper frames, of the Queen and the Prince of Wales. They looked down on the performance, and, to my thinking, seemed to heighten the grotesqueness of it all.

Just when the silence was getting unendurable, the body turned over and rolled away from the basin to the side of the room, where it lay stomach-up. There was a faint 'plop' from the basin – exactly like the noise a fish makes when it takes a fly – and the green light in the centre revived.

I looked at the basin, and saw, bobbing in the water, the dried, shrivelled, black head of a native baby – open eyes, open mouth, and shaved scalp. It was worse, being so very sudden, than the crawling exhibition. We had no time to say anything before it began to speak.

Read Poe's account of the voice that came from the mesmerized dying man, and you will realize less than one-half of the horror of that head's voice.

There was an interval of a second or two between each word, and a sort of 'ring, ring, ring', in the note of the voice, like the timbre of a bell. It pealed slowly, as if talking to itself, for several minutes before I got rid of my cold sweat. Then the blessed solution struck me. I looked at the body lying near the doorway, and saw, just where the hollow of the throat joins on the shoulders, a muscle that had nothing to do with any man's regular breathing twitching away steadily. The whole thing was a careful reproduction of the Egyptian teraphim that one reads about sometimes; and the voice was as clever and as appalling a piece of ventriloquism as one could wish to hear. All this time the head was 'lip-lip-lapping' against the side of the basin, and speaking. It told Suddhoo, on his face again whining, of his son's illness and of the state of the illness up to the evening of that very night. I always shall respect the seal-cutter for keeping so faithfully to the time of the Peshawur telegrams. It went on to say that skilled doctors were night and day watching over the man's life; and that he would eventually recover if the fee to the potent sorcerer, whose servant was the head in the basin, were doubled.

Here the mistake from the artistic point of view came in. To ask for twice your stipulated fee in a voice that Lazarus might have used when he rose from the dead, is absurd. Janoo, who is really a woman of masculine intellect, saw this as quickly as I did. I heard her say, '*Asli nahin! Fareib!*' scornfully under her breath; and just as she said so, the light in the basin died out, the head stopped talking, and we heard the room door creak on its hinges. Then Janoo struck a match, lit the lamp, and we saw that the head, basin, and seal-cutter were gone. Suddhoo was wringing his hands, and explaining to anyone who cared to listen that, if his chances of eternal salvation depended on it, he could not raise another two hundred rupees. Azizun was nearly in hysterics in the corner; while Janoo sat down composedly on one of his beds to discuss the probabilities of the whole thing being a *bunao*, or 'make-up'.

I explained as much as I knew of the seal-cutter's way of

jadoo; but her argument was much more simple. 'The magic that is always demanding gifts is no true magic,' said she. 'My mother told me that the only potent love-spells are those which are told you for love. This seal-cutter man is a liar and a devil. I dare not tell, do anything, or get anything done, because I am in debt to Bhagwan Dass the *bunnia* for two gold rings and a heavy anklet. I must get my food from his shop. The seal-cutter is the friend of Bhagwan Dass, and he would poison my food. A fool's *jadoo* has been going on for ten days, and has cost Suddhoo many rupees each night. The seal-cutter used black hens and lemons and charms before. He never showed us anything like this till to-night. Azizun is a fool, and will be a *purdah-nashin* soon. Suddhoo has lost his strength and lost his wits. See now! I had hoped to get from Suddhoo many rupees while he lived, and many more after his death; and behold, he is spending everything on that offspring of a devil and a she-ass, the seal-cutter!'

Here I said, 'But what induced Suddhoo to drag *me* into the business? Of course I can speak to the seal-cutter, and he shall refund. The whole thing is child's talk – shame – and senseless.'

'Suddhoo *is* an old child,' said Janoo. 'He has lived on the roofs these seventy years and is as senseless as a milch-goat. He brought you here to assure himself that he was not breaking any law of the Sirkar, whose salt he ate many years ago. He worships the dust off the feet of the seal-cutter, and that cow-devourer has forbidden him to go and see his son. What does Suddhoo know of your laws or the lightning-post? *I* have to watch his money going day by day to that lying beast below.'

Janoo stamped her foot on the floor and nearly cried with vexation; while Suddhoo was whimpering under a blanket in the corner, and Azizun was trying to guide the pipe-stem to his foolish old mouth.

Now, the case stands thus. Unthinkingly, I have laid myself open to the charge of aiding and abetting the seal-cutter in obtaining money under false pretences, which is forbidden by Section 420 of the Indian Penal Code. I am helpless in the matter for these reasons. I cannot inform the Police. What witnesses would support my statement? Janoo refuses flatly, and Azizun is a married woman somewhere near Bareilly – lost in this big India of ours. I dare not again take the law into my own hands, and speak to the seal-cutter; for certain am I that, not only would Suddhoo disbelieve me, but this step would end in the poisoning of Janoo, who is bound hand and foot by her debt to the *bunnia*. Suddhoo is an old dotard; and whenever we meet mumbles my idiotic joke that the Sirkar rather patronizes the Black Art than otherwise. His son is well now; but Suddhoo is completely under the influence of the seal-cutter, by whose advice he regulates the affairs of his life. Janoo watches daily the money that she hoped to wheedle out of Suddhoo taken by the seal-cutter and becomes daily more furious and sullen.

She will never tell, because she dare not; but, unless something happens to prevent her, I am afraid that the seal-cutter will die of cholera – the white arsenic kind – about the middle of May. And thus I shall be privy to a murder in the House of Suddhoo!

The Bisara of Pooree

Little Blind Fish, thou art marvellous wise,
Little Blind Fish, who put out thy eyes?
Open thy ears while I whisper my wish –
Bring me a lover, thou little Blind Fish.

The Charm of the Bisara

Some natives say that it came from the other side of Kulu, where the eleven-inch Temple Sapphire is. Others that it was made at the Devil-Shrine of Ao-Chung in Tibet, was stolen by a Kafir, from him by a Gurkha, from him again by a Lahouli, from him by a *khitmutgar*, and by this latter sold to an Englishman, so all its virtue was lost; because, to work properly, the Bisara of Pooree must be stolen – with bloodshed if possible, but, at any rate, stolen.

These stories of the coming into India are all false. It was made at Pooree ages since – the manner of its making would fill a small book – was stolen by one of the Temple dancing-girls there, for her own purposes, and then passed on from hand to hand, steadily northward, till it reached Hanlé; always bearing the same name – the Bisara of Pooree. In shape it is a tiny square box of silver, studded outside with eight small balas-rubies. Inside the box, which opens with a spring, is a little eyeless fish, carved from some sort of dark, shiny nut and wrapped in a shred of faded gold cloth. That is the Bisara of Pooree, and it were better for a man to take a king-cobra in his hand than to touch the Bisara of Pooree.

All kinds of magic are out of date and done away with, except in India, where nothing changes in spite of the shiny, top-scum stuff that people call 'civilization'. Any man who know about the Bisara of Pooree will tell you what its powers are – always supposing that it has been honestly stolen. It is the only regularly working, trustworthy love-charm in the country, with one exception. (The other charm is in the hands of a trooper of the Nizam's Horse, at a place called Tuprani, due north of Hyderabad.) This can be depended upon for a fact. Some one else may explain it.

If the Bisara be not stolen, but given or bought or found, it turns against its owner in three years, and leads to ruin or death. This is another fact which you may explain when you have time. Meanwhile, you can laugh at it. At present the Bisara is safe on a hack-pony's neck, inside the blue bead-necklace that keeps off the Evil Eye. If the pony-driver ever finds it, and wears it, or gives it to his wife, I am sorry for him.

A very dirty Hill-coolie woman, with goitre, owned it at Theog in 1884. It came into Simla from the North before Churton's *khitmutgar* bought it, and sold it, for three times its silver-value, to Churton, who collected curiosities. The servant knew no more what he had bought than the master; but a man looking over Churton's collection of curiosities – Churton was an Assistant Commissioner, by the way – saw, and held his tongue. He was an Englishman, but knew how to believe. Which shows that he was different from most Englishmen. He knew that it was dangerous to have any share in the little box when working or dormant; for Love unsought is a terrible gift.

Pack – 'Grubby' Pack, as we used to call him – was, in every way, a nasty little man who must have crawled into the Army by mistake. He was three inches taller than his sword, but not half so strong. And the sword was a fifty-shilling, tailor-made one. Nobody liked him, and, I suppose, it was his wizenedness and worthlessness that made him fall so hopelessly in love with Miss Hollis, who was good and sweet, and five feet seven in her tennis-shoes. He was not content with falling in love quietly, but brought all the strength of his miserable little nature into the business. If he had not been so objectionable, one might have pitied him. He vapoured, and fretted, and fumed, and trotted up and down, and tried to make himself pleasing in Miss Hollis's big, quiet, grey eyes, and failed. It was one of the cases that you sometimes meet, even in our country, where we marry by Code, of a really blind attachment all on one side, without the faintest possibility of return. Miss Hollis looked on Pack as some sort of vermin running about the road. He had no prospects beyond Captain's pay, and no wits to help that out by one penny. In a large-sized man love like his would have been touching. In a good man it would have been grand. He being what he was, it was only a nuisance.

You will believe this much. What you will not believe is what follows: Churton, and The Man who Knew what the Bisara was, were lunching at the Simla Club together. Churton was complaining of life in general. His best mare had rolled out of stable down the cliff and had broken her back; his decisions were being reversed by the upper Courts more than an Assistant Commissioner of eight years' standing has a right to expect; he knew liver and fever, and for weeks past had felt out of sorts. Altogether, he was disgusted and disheartened.

Simla Club dining-room is built, as all the world knows, in two sections, with an arch-arrangement dividing them. Come in, turn to your own left, take the table under the window, and you cannot see any one who has come in, turned to the right, and taken a table on the right side of the arch. Curiously enough, every word that you say can be heard, not only by the other diner, but by the servants beyond the screen through which they bring dinner. This is worth knowing. An echoing-room is a trap to be forewarned against.

Half in fun, and half hoping to be believed, The Man who Knew told Churton the story of the Bisara of Pooree at rather greater length than I have told it to you in this place; winding up with a suggestion that Churton might as well throw the little box down the hill and see whether all his troubles would go with it. In ordinary ears, English ears, the tale was only an interesting bit of folklore. Churton laughed, said that he felt better for his tiffin, and went out. Pack had been tiffining by himself to the right of the arch, and had heard everything. He was nearly mad with his absurd infatuation for Miss Hollis, that all Simla had been laughing about.

It is a curious thing that, when a man hates or loves beyond reason, he is ready to go beyond reason to gratify his feelings; which he would not do for money or power merely. Depend upon it, Solomon would never have built altars to Ashtaroth and all those ladies with queer names, if there had not been trouble of some kind in his zenana, and nowhere else. But this is beside the story. The facts of the case are these: Pack called on Churton next day when Churton was out, left his card, and stole the Bisara of Pooree from its place under the clock on the mantelpiece! Stole it like the thief he was by nature! Three day later, all Simla was electrified by the news that Miss Hollis had accepted Pack – the shrivelled rat, Pack! Do you desire clearer evidence than this? The Bisara of Pooree had been stolen, and it worked as it had always done when won by foul means.

There are three or four times in a man's life when he is justified in meddling with other people's affairs to play Providence.

The Man who Knew felt that he was justified; but believing and acting on a belief are quite different things. The insolent satisfaction of Pack as he ambled by the side of Miss Hollis, and Churton's striking release from liver, as soon as the Bisara of Pooree had gone, decided The Man. He explained to Churton, and Churton laughed, because he was not brought up to believe that men on the Government House List steal – at least little things. But the miraculous acceptance by Miss Hollis of that tailor, Pack, decided him to take steps on suspicion. He vowed that he only wanted to find out where his ruby-studded silver box had vanished to. You cannot accuse a man on the Government House List of stealing; and if you rifle his room, you are a thief yourself. Churton, prompted by The Man who Knew, decided on burglary. If he found nothing in Pack's room . . . But it is not nice to think of what would have happened in that case.

Pack went to a dance at Benmore – Benmore was Benmore in those days, and not an office – and danced fifteen waltzes out of twenty-two with Miss Hollis. Churton and The Man took all the keys that they could lay hands on, and went to Pack's room in the hotel, certain that his servants would be away. Pack was a cheap soul. He had not purchased a decent cash-box to keep his papers in, but one of those native imitations that you buy for ten rupees. It opened to any sort of key, and there at the bottom, under Pack's Insurance Policy, lay the Bisara of Pooree!

Churton called Pack names, put the Bisara of Poore in his pocket, and went to the dance with The Man. At least, he came in time for supper, and saw the beginning of the end in Miss Hollis's eyes. She was hysterical after supper, and was taken away by her Mamma.

At the dance, with the abominable Bisara in his pocket, Churton twisted his foot on one of the steps leading down to the old Rink, and had to be sent home in a 'rickshaw, grumbling. He did not believe in the Bisara of Pooree any the more for this manifestation, but he sought out Pack and called him some ugly names; and 'thief' was the mildest of them. Pack took the names with the nervous smile of a little man who wants both soul and body to resent an insult, and went his way. There was no public scandal.

A week later Pack got his definite dismissal from Miss Hollis. There had been a mistake in the placing of her affections, she said. So he went away to Madras, where he can do no great harm even if he lives to be a Colonel.

Churton insisted upon The Man who Knew taking the Bisara of Pooree as a gift. The Man took it, went down to the Cart-Road at once, found a cart-pony with a blue bead-necklace, fastened the Bisara of Pooree inside the necklace with a piece of shoe-string and thanked Heaven that he was rid of a danger. Remember, in case you ever find it, that you must not destroy the Bisara of Pooree. I have not time to explain why just now, but the power lies in the little wooden fish. Mr Gubernatis or Max Müller could tell you more about it than I.

You will say that all this story is made up. Very well. If ever you come across a little, silver, ruby-studded box, seven-eighths of an inch long by three-quarters wide, with a dark-brown wooden fish, wrapped in gold cloth, inside it, keep it. Keep it for three years, and then you will discover for yourself whether my story is true or false.

Better still, steal it as Pack did, and you will be sorry that you had not killed yourself in the beginning.

The Gate of the Hundred Sorrows

If I can attain Heaven for a pice, why should you be envious?

Opium Smoker's Proverb

This is no work of mine. My friend, Gabral Misquitta, the half-caste, spoke it all, between moonset and morning, six weeks before he died; and I took it down from his mouth as he answered my questions. So: –

It lies between the Coppersmith's Gully and the pipe-stem sellers' quarter, within a hundred yards, too, as the crow files, of the Mosque of Wazir Khan. I don't mind telling any one this much, but I defy him to find the Gate, however well he may think he knows the City. You might even go through the very gully it stands in a hundred times, and be none the wiser. We used to call the gully 'The Gully of the Black Smoke', but its native name is altogether different, of course. A loaded donkey couldn't pass between the walls; and, at one point, just before you reach the Gate, a bulged house-front makes people go along all sideways.

It isn't really a gate, though. It's a house. Old Fung-Tching had it first five years ago. He was a boot-maker in Calcutta. They say that he murdered his wife there when he was drunk. That was why he dropped bazar-rum and took to the Black Smoke instead. Later on, he came up north and opened the

Gate as a house where you could get your smoke in peace and quiet. Mind you, it was a *pukka*, respectable opium-house, and not one of those stifling, sweltering *chandoo-khanas* that you can find all over the City. No; the old man knew his business thoroughly, and he was most clean for a Chinaman. He was a one-eyed little chap, not much more than five feet high, and both his middle fingers were gone. All the same, he was the handiest man at rolling black pills I have ever seen. Never seemed to be touched by the Smoke, either; and what he took day and night, night and day, was a caution. I've been at it five years, and I can do my fair share of the Smoke with any one; but I was a child to Fung-Tching that way. All the same, the old man was keen on his money; very keen; and that's what I can't understand. I heard he saved a good deal before he died, but his nephew has got all that now; and the old man's gone back to China to be buried.

He kept the big upper room, where his best customers gathered, as neat as a new pin. In one corner used to stand Fung-Tching's Joss – almost as ugly as Fung-Tching – and there were always sticks burning under his nose; but you never smelt 'em when the pipes were going thick. Opposite the Joss was Fung-Tching's coffin. He had spent a good deal of his savings on that, and whenever a new man came to the Gate he was always introduced to it. It was lacquered black, with red and gold writings on it, and I've heard that Fung-Tching brought it out all the way from China. I don't know whether that's true or not, but I know that, if I came first in the evening, I used to spread my mat just at the foot of it. It was a quiet corner, you see, and a sort of breeze from the gully came in at the window now and then. Besides the mats, there was no other furniture in the room – only the coffin, and the old Joss all green and blue and purple with age and polish.

Fung-Tching never told us why he called the place 'The Gate of the Hundred Sorrows'. (He was the only Chinaman I know who used bad-sounding fancy names. Most of them are flowery. As you'll see in Calcutta.) We used to find that out for ourselves. Nothing grows on you so much, if you're white, as the Black Smoke. A yellow man is made different. Opium doesn't tell on him scarcely at all; but white and black suffer a good deal. Of course, there are some people that the Smoke doesn't touch any more than tobacco would at first. They just doze a bit, as one would fall asleep naturally, and next morning they are almost fit for work. Now, I was one of that sort when I began, but I've been at it for five years pretty steadily, and it's different now. There was an old aunt of mine, down Agra way, and she left me a little at her death. About sixty rupees a month secured. Sixty isn't much. I can recollect a time, seems hundreds and hundreds of years ago, that I was getting my three hundred a month, and pickings, when I was working on a big timber-contract in Calcutta.

I didn't stick to that work for long. The Black Smoke does not allow of much other business; and even though I am very little affected by it, as men go, I couldn't do a day's work now to save my life. After all, sixty rupees is what I want. When old Fung-Tching was alive he used to draw the money for me, give me about half of it to live on (I eat very little), and the rest he kept himself. I was free of the Gate at any time of the day and night, and could smoke and sleep there when I liked; so I didn't care. I know the old man made a good thing out of it; but that's no matter. Nothing matters much to me; and besides, the money always came fresh and fresh each month.

There was ten of us met at the Gate when the place was first opened. Me, and two Babus from a Government Office somewhere in Anarkulli, but they got the sack and couldn't pay (no man who has to work in the daylight can do the Black Smoke for any length of time straight on); a Chinaman that was Fung-Tching's nephew; a bazar-woman that had got a lot of money somehow; an English loafer – MacSomebody, I think, but I have forgotten, – that smoked heaps, but never seemed to pay anything (they said he had saved Fung-Tching's life at some trial in Calcutta when he was barrister); another Eurasian, like myself, from Madras; a half-caste woman, and a couple of men who said they had come from the North. I think they must have been Persians or Afghans or something. There are not more than five of us living now, but we come regular. I don't know what happened to the Babus; but the bazar-woman, she died after six months of the Gate, and I think Fung-Tching took her bangles and nose-ring for himself. But I'm not certain. The Englishman, he drank as well as smoked, and he dropped off. One of the Persians got killed in a row at night by the big well near the mosque a long time ago, and the Police shut up the well, because they said it was full of foul air. They found him dead at the bottom of it. So, you see, there is only me, the Chinaman, the half-caste woman that we call the Memsahib (she used to live with Fung-Tching), the other Eurasian, and one of the Persians. The Memsahib looks very old now. I think she was a young woman when the Gate was opened; but we are all old for the matter of that. Hundreds and hundreds of years old. It's very hard to keep count of time in the Gate, and, besides, time doesn't matter to me. I draw my sixty rupees fresh and fresh every month. A very, very long while ago, when I used to be getting three hundred and fifty rupees a month, and pickings, on a big timber-contract at Calcutta, I had a wife of sorts. But she's dead now. People said that I killed her by taking to the Black Smoke. Perhaps I did, but it's so long since that it doesn't matter. Sometimes, when I first came to the Gate, I used to feel sorry for it; but that's all over and done with long ago, and I draw my sixty rupees fresh and fresh every month, and am quite happy. Not *drunk* happy, you know, but always quiet and soothed and contented.

How did I take to it? It began at Calcutta. I used to try it in my own house, just to see what it was like. I never went very far, but I think my wife must have died then. Anyhow, I found myself here, and got to know Fung-Tching. I don't remember rightly how that came about; but he told me of the Gate and I used to go there, and, somehow, I have never got away from it since. Mind you, though, the Gate was a respectable place in Fung-Tching's time, where you could be comfortable, and not at all like the *chandoo-khanas* where the niggers go. No; it was clean, and quiet, and not crowded. Of course, there were others besides us ten and the man; but we always had a mat apiece, with a wadded woollen head-piece, all covered with black and red dragons and things, just like the coffin in the corner.

At the end of one's third pipe the dragons used to move

about and fight. I've watched 'em many and many a night through. I used to regulate my Smoke that way, and now it takes a dozen pipes to make 'em stir. Besides, they are all torn and dirty, like the mats, and old Fung-Tching is dead. He died a couple of years ago, and gave me the pipe I always use now – a silver one, with queer beasts crawling up and down the receiver-bottle below the cup. Before that, I think, I used a big bamboo stem with a copper cup, a very small one, and a green jade mouthpiece. It was a little thicker than a walking-stick stem, and smoked sweet, very sweet. The bamboo seemed to suck up the smoke. Silver doesn't, and I've got to clean it out now and then; that's a great deal of trouble, but I smoke it for the old man's sake. He must have made a good thing out of me, but he always gave me clean mats and pillows, and the best stuff you could get anywhere.

When he died, his nephew Tsin-ling took up the Gate, and he called it the 'Temple of the Three Possessions', but we old ones speak of it as the 'Hundred Sorrows', all the same. The nephew does things very shabbily, and I think the Memsahib must help him. She lives with him; same as she used to do with the old man. The two let in all sorts of low people, niggers and all, and the Black Smoke isn't as good as it used to be. I've found burnt bran in my pipe over and over again. The old man would have died if that had happened in his time. Besides, the room is never cleaned, and all the mats are torn and cut at the edges. The coffin is gone – gone to China again – with the old man and two ounces of Smoke inside it, in case he should want 'em on the way.

The Joss doesn't get so many sticks burnt under his nose

as he used to. That's a sign of ill-luck, as sure as death. He's all brown, too, and no one ever attends to him. That's the Memsahib's work, I know; because, when Tsin-ling tried to burn gilt paper before him, she said it was a waste of money, and, if he kept a stick burning very slowly, the Joss wouldn't know the difference. So now we've got the sticks mixed with a lot of glue, and they take half an hour longer to burn, and smell stinky. Let alone the smell of the room by itself. No business can get on if they try that sort of thing. The Joss doesn't like it. I can see that. Late at night, sometimes, he turns all sorts of queer colours – blue and green and red – just as he used to do when old Fung-Tching was alive; and he rolls his eyes and stamps his feet like a devil.

I don't know why I don't leave the place and smoke quietly in a little room of my own in the bazar. Most like, Tsin-ling would kill me if I went away – he draws my sixty rupees now – and besides, it's too much trouble, and I've grown to be very fond of the Gate. It's not much to look at. Not what it was in the old man's time, but I couldn't leave it. I've seen so many come in and out. And I've seen so many die here on the mats that I should be afraid of dying in the open now. I've seen some things that people would call strange enough; but nothing is strange when you're on the Black Smoke, except the Black Smoke. And if it was, it wouldn't matter.

Fung-Tching used to be very particular about his people, and never got in any one who'd give trouble by dying messy and such. But the nephew isn't half so careful. He tells everywhere that he keeps a 'first-chop' house. Never tries to get men in quietly, and make them comfortable like Fung-Tching did. That's why the Gate is getting a little bit more known than it used to be. Among the niggers of course. The nephew daren't get a white, or, for matter of that, a mixed skin into the place. He has to keep us three, of course – me and the Memsahib and the other Eurasian. We're fixtures. But he wouldn't give us credit for a pipeful – not for anything.

One of these days, I hope, I shall die in the Gate. The Persian and the Madras man are terribly shaky now. They've got a boy to light their pipes for them. I always do that myself. Most like, I shall see them carried out before me. I don't think I shall ever outlive the Memsahib or Tsin-ling. Women last longer than men at the Black Smoke, and Tsin-ling has a deal of the old man's blood in him, though he does smoke cheap stuff. The bazar-woman knew when she was going two days before her time; and she died on a clean mat with a nicely-wadded pillow, and the old man hung up her pipe just above the Joss. He was always fond of her, I fancy. But he took her bangles just the same.

I should like to die like the bazar-woman – on a clean, cool mat with a pipe of good stuff between my lips. When I feel I'm going, I shall ask Tsin-ling for them, and he can draw my sixty rupees a month, fresh and fresh, as long as he pleases. Then I shall lie back, quiet and comfortable, and watch the black and red dragons have their last big fight together; and then . . .

Well, it doesn't matter. Nothing matters much to me – only I wish Tsin-ling wouldn't put bran into the Black Smoke.

The Story of Muhammad Din

> Who is the happy man? He that sees, in his own house at home, little children crowned with dust, leaping and falling and crying.
>
> *Munichandra*, translated by Professor Peterson

The polo-ball was an old one, scarred, chipped, and dinted. It stood on the mantelpiece among the pipe-stems which Imam Din, *khitmutgar*, was cleaning for me.

'Does the Heaven-born want this ball?' said Imam Din deferentially.

The Heaven-born set no particular store by it; but of what use was a polo-ball to a *khitmutgar*?

'By Your Honour's favour, I have a little son. He has seen this ball, and desires it to play with. I do not want it for myself.'

No one would for an instant accuse portly old Imam Din of wanting to play with polo-balls. He carried out the battered thing into the veranda; and there followed a hurricane of joyful squeaks, a patter of small feet, and the *thud-thud-thud* of the ball rolling along the ground. Evidently the little son had been waiting outside the door to secure his treasure. But how had he managed to see that polo-ball?

Next day, coming back from office half an hour earlier than usual, I was aware of a small figure in the dining-room – a tiny, plump figure in a ridiculously inadequate shirt which came, perhaps, half-way down the tubby stomach. It wandered round the room, thumb in mouth, crooning to itself as it took stock of the pictures. Undoubtedly this was the 'little son'.

He had no business in my room, of course; but was so deeply absorbed in his discoveries that he never noticed me in the doorway. I stepped into the room and startled him nearly into a fit. He sat down on the ground with a gasp. His eyes opened, and his mouth followed suit. I knew what was coming, and fled, followed by a long, dry howl which reached the servants' quarters far more quickly than any command of mine had ever done. In ten seconds Imam Din was in the dining-room. Then despairing sobs arose, and I returned to find Imam Din admonishing the small sinner, who was using most of his shirt as a handkerchief.

'This boy,' said Imam Din judicially, 'is a *budmash* – a big *budmash*. He will, without doubt, go to the *jail-khana* for his behaviour.' Renewed yells from the penitent, and an elaborate apology to myself from Imam Din.

'Tell the baby,' said I, 'that the Sahib is not angry, and take him away.' Imam Din conveyed my forgiveness to the offender, who had now gathered all his shirt round his neck, stringwise, and the yell subsided into a sob. The two set off for the door. 'His name,' said Imam Din, as though the name were part of the crime, 'is Muhammad Din, and he is a *budmash*.' Freed from present danger, Muhammad Din turned round in his father's arms, and said gravely, 'It is true that my name is Muhammad Din, Tahib, but I am not a *budmash*. I am a *man*!'

From that day dated my acquaintance with Muhammad Din. Never again did he come into my dining-room, but on the neutral ground of the garden we greeted each other with much state, though our conversation was confined to 'Talaam, Tahib' from his side, and 'Salaam, Muhammad Din' from mine. Daily on my return from office, the little white shirt and the fat little body used to rise from the shade of the creeper-covered trellis where they had been hid; and daily I checked my horse here, that my salutation might not be slurred over or given unseemly.

Muhammad Din never had any companions. He used to trot about the compound, in and out of the castor-oil bushes, on mysterious errands of his own. One day I stumbled upon some of his handiwork far down the grounds. He had half buried the polo-ball in dust, and stuck six shrivelled old marigold flowers in a circle round it. Outside that circle again was a rude square, traced out in bits of red brick alternating with fragments of broken china; the whole bounded by a little bank of dust. The water-man from the well-curb put in a plea for the small architect, saying that it was only the play of a baby and did not much disfigure my garden.

Heaven knows that I had no intention of touching the child's work then or later; but that evening, a stroll through the garden brought me unawares full on it; so that I trampled, before I knew, marigold-heads, dust-bank, and fragments of broken soap-dish into confusion past all hope of mending. Next morning, I came upon Muhammad Din crying softly to himself over the ruin I had wrought. Some one had cruelly told him that the Sahib was very angry with him for spoiling the garden, and had scattered his rubbish, using bad language the while. Muhammad Din laboured for an hour at effacing every trace of the dusk-bank and pottery fragments, and it was with a tearful and apologetic facc that he said, 'Talaam, Tahib,' when I came home from office. A hasty inquiry resulted in Imam Din informing Muhammad Din that, by my singular favour, he was permitted to disport himself as he pleased. Whereat the child took heart and fell to tracing the ground-plan of an edifice which was to eclipse the marigold-polo-ball creation.

For some months the chubby little eccentricity revolved in his humble orbit among the castor-oil bushes and in the dust; always fashioning magnificent palaces from stale flowers thrown away by the bearer, smooth water-worn pebbles, bits of broken glass, and feathers pulled, I fancy, from my fowls – always alone, and always crooning to himself.

A gaily-spotted sea-shell was dropped one day close to the last of his little buildings; and I looked that Muhammad Din should build something more than ordinarily splendid on the strength of it. Nor was I disappointed. He meditated for the better part of an hour, and his crooning rose to a jubilant song. Then he began tracing in the dust. It would certainly be a wondrous palace, this one, for it was two yards long and a yard broad in ground-plan. But the palace was never completed.

Next day there was no Muhammad Din at the head of the carriage-drive, and no 'Talaam, Tahib' to welcome my return. I had grown accustomed to the greeting, and its omission troubled me. Next day Imam Din told me that the child was suffering slightly from fever and needed quinine. He got the medicine, and an English Doctor.

'They have no stamina, these brats,' said the Doctor, as he left Imam Din's quarters.

A week later, though I would have given much to have avoided it, I met on the road to the Mussulman burying-ground Imam Din, accompanied by one other friend, carrying in his arms, wrapped in a white cloth, all that was left of little Muhammad Din.

1. BOCCACCIO · *Mrs Rosie and the Priest*
2. GERARD MANLEY HOPKINS · *As kingfishers catch fire*
3. *The Saga of Gunnlaug Serpent-tongue*
4. THOMAS DE QUINCEY · *On Murder Considered as One of the Fine Arts*
5. FRIEDRICH NIETZSCHE · *Aphorisms on Love and Hate*
6. JOHN RUSKIN · *Traffic*
7. PU SONGLING · *Wailing Ghosts*
8. JONATHAN SWIFT · *A Modest Proposal*
9. *Three Tang Dynasty Poets*
10. WALT WHITMAN · *On the Beach at Night Alone*
11. KENKŌ · *A Cup of Sake Beneath the Cherry Trees*
12. BALTASAR GRACIÁN · *How to Use Your Enemies*
13. JOHN KEATS · *The Eve of St Agnes*
14. THOMAS HARDY · *Woman much missed*
15. GUY DE MAUPASSANT · *Femme Fatale*
16. MARCO POLO · *Travels in the Land of Serpents and Pearls*
17. SUETONIUS · *Caligula*
18. APOLLONIUS OF RHODES · *Jason and Medea*
19. ROBERT LOUIS STEVENSON · *Olalla*
20. KARL MARX AND FRIEDRICH ENGELS · *The Communist Manifesto*
21. PETRONIUS · *Trimalchio's Feast*
22. JOHANN PETER HEBEL · *How a Ghastly Story Was Brought to Light by a Common or Garden Butcher's Dog*
23. HANS CHRISTIAN ANDERSEN · *The Tinder Box*
24. RUDYARD KIPLING · *The Gate of the Hundred Sorrows*
25. DANTE · *Circles of Hell*
26. HENRY MAYHEW · *Of Street Piemen*
27. HAFEZ · *The nightingales are drunk*
28. GEOFFREY CHAUCER · *The Wife of Bath*
29. MICHEL DE MONTAIGNE · *How We Weep and Laugh at the Same Thing*
30. THOMAS NASHE · *The Terrors of the Night*
31. EDGAR ALLAN POE · *The Tell-Tale Heart*
32. MARY KINGSLEY · *A Hippo Banquet*
33. JANE AUSTEN · *The Beautifull Cassandra*
34. ANTON CHEKHOV · *Gooseberries*
35. SAMUEL TAYLOR COLERIDGE · *Well, they are gone, and here must I remain*
36. JOHANN WOLFGANG VON GOETHE · *Sketchy, Doubtful, Incomplete Jottings*
37. CHARLES DICKENS · *The Great Winglebury Duel*
38. HERMAN MELVILLE · *The Maldive Shark*
39. ELIZABETH GASKELL · *The Old Nurse's Story*
40. NIKOLAY LESKOV · *The Steel Flea*

41. HONORÉ DE BALZAC · *The Atheist's Mass*
42. CHARLOTTE PERKINS GILMAN · *The Yellow Wall-Paper*
43. C.P. CAVAFY · *Remember, Body . . .*
44. FYODOR DOSTOEVSKY · *The Meek One*
45. GUSTAVE FLAUBERT · *A Simple Heart*
46. NIKOLAI GOGOL · *The Nose*
47. SAMUEL PEPYS · *The Great Fire of London*
48. EDITH WHARTON · *The Reckoning*
49. HENRY JAMES · *The Figure in the Carpet*
50. WILFRED OWEN · *Anthem For Doomed Youth*
51. WOLFGANG AMADEUS MOZART · *My Dearest Father*
52. PLATO · *Socrates' Defence*
53. CHRISTINA ROSSETTI · *Goblin Market*
54. *Sindbad the Sailor*
55. SOPHOCLES · *Antigone*
56. RYŪNOSUKE AKUTAGAWA · *The Life of a Stupid Man*
57. LEO TOLSTOY · *How Much Land Does A Man Need?*
58. GIORGIO VASARI · *Leonardo da Vinci*
59. OSCAR WILDE · *Lord Arthur Savile's Crime*
60. SHEN FU · *The Old Man of the Moon*
61. AESOP · *The Dolphins, the Whales and the Gudgeon*
62. MATSUO BASHŌ · *Lips too Chilled*
63. EMILY BRONTË · *The Night is Darkening Round Me*
64. JOSEPH CONRAD · *To-morrow*
65. RICHARD HAKLUYT · *The Voyage of Sir Francis Drake Around the Whole Globe*
66. KATE CHOPIN · *A Pair of Silk Stockings*
67. CHARLES DARWIN · *It was snowing butterflies*
68. BROTHERS GRIMM · *The Robber Bridegroom*
69. CATULLUS · *I Hate and I Love*
70. HOMER · *Circe and the Cyclops*
71. D. H. LAWRENCE · *Il Duro*
72. KATHERINE MANSFIELD · *Miss Brill*
73. OVID · *The Fall of Icarus*
74. SAPPHO · *Come Close*
75. IVAN TURGENEV · *Kasyan from the Beautiful Lands*
76. VIRGIL · *O Cruel Alexis*
77. H. G. WELLS · *A Slip under the Microscope*
78. HERODOTUS · *The Madness of Cambyses*
79. *Speaking of Siva*
80. *The Dhammapada*